Baseball was, is and always will be to me
the best game in the world.

– Babe Ruth

Kane Miller, A Division of EDC Publishing

Text and illustrations copyright © Richard Torrey 2012

Library of Congress Control Number: 2010943438

Manufactured by Regent Publishing Services, Hong Kong
Printed September 2011 in ShenZhen, Guangdong, China

ISBN: 978-1-61067-054-8

1 2 3 4 5 6 7 8 9 10

A BASEBALL Story

By Richard Torrey

SWOOSH

CRACK!

Kane Miller

A DIVISION OF EDC PUBLISHING

Jingle-Jingle-Jingle!
That's the sound of the ice cream man.
But I'm not thinking about ice cream,
I'm thinking about baseball.
That's because today is my team's first game
of the season, and I have to get ready!

Not now.

Are you getting ice cream, Jordan?

Before the game, I put on my uniform.
My hat and my jersey have big stars on them.
(My team is called the Stars.)
I also wear bumpy shoes called cleats to help me run faster.

I'm almost ready to go, but first I have to look in the mirror to make sure I look like a real baseball player.

Yup!

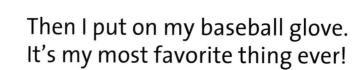

Then I put on my baseball glove.
It's my most favorite thing ever!

When I wear it, I always have to put it
up to my face because it smells so good.

My coach's name is Mr. Hanes, but we call him "Coach Mike."

Hi, Coach Mike!

Before the game, Coach Mike tells us that baseball players always have to be ready.

And we are!

We practice our throwing.

We practice our catching.

Then it's time to play ball!

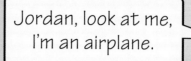

The other team gets to bat first,
so I run my fastest to the outfield.

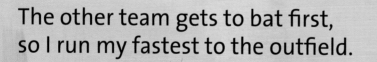

My mom and dad are waving, but I can't wave back because I have to be ready like Coach Mike says.

In the outfield, you have to try to catch
the ball if they hit it near you.

When you catch it, it's called an out.

I like when it's our turn to bat. We get to run our fastest off the field and even get a drink.

Before you can bat, you have to put on a special batting helmet, just like the real baseball players wear.

When it's my turn to bat, I walk to home plate. My mom and dad are waving again, but I still can't wave back because I have to be ready.

If you want to get a hit, you have to watch the ball really, really, hard. Then you have to swing the bat your fastest ever!

When you miss, the umpire calls "STRIKE!" to tell everyone that you didn't get a hit.

CRACK!

But when you get a hit, he doesn't say anything, since everyone already knows you got a hit.

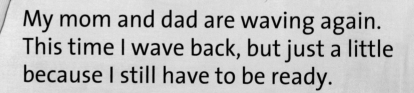

My mom and dad are waving again. This time I wave back, but just a little because I still have to be ready.

Getting a hit is fun, but it's even more fun when you score a run. Everyone cheers for you. It feels good – like it's your birthday or something.

When the game is over, we shake hands with the other team and say, "Good game."

Then he tells us that baseball players
always have to be ready ...

JINGLE JINGLE JINGLE

... for ice cream!

ICE CREAM

And we are!